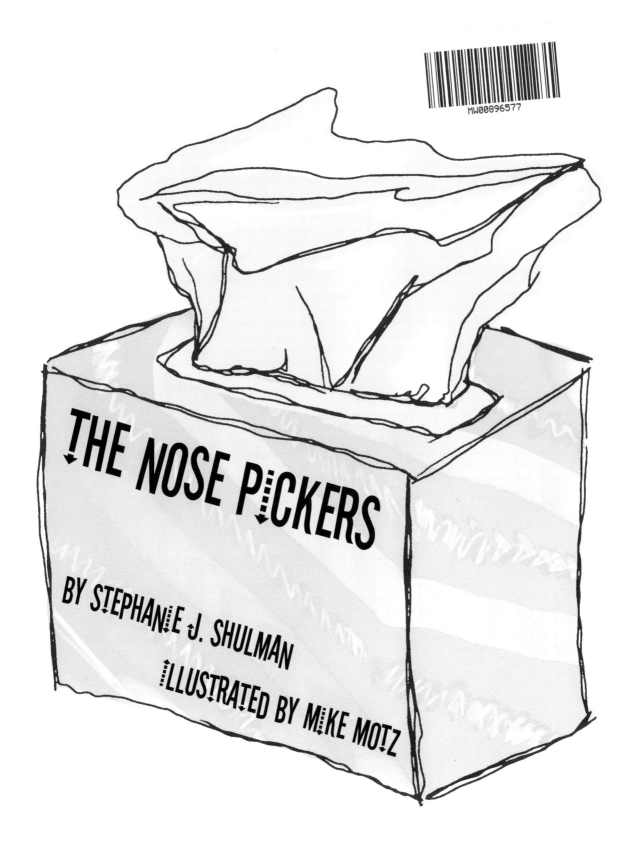

THE NOSE PICKERS

BY STEPHANIE J. SHULMAN

ILLUSTRATED BY MIKE MOTZ

Lillian Blanche Books, Inc.
New York

– M.M.

Jake and Jesse,
I picked this one for you. – S.S.

STARTS NOW ⟶

The Nose Pickers
©2012 by Stephanie J. Shulman
Lillian Blanche Books, Inc.

www.LillianBlancheBooks.com

ISBN: 978-0-9841794-1-1
LCCN: 2012901455

Fonts: Stereofidelic and Minya Nouvelle, Typodermic Fonts Larabie Fonts Collection.

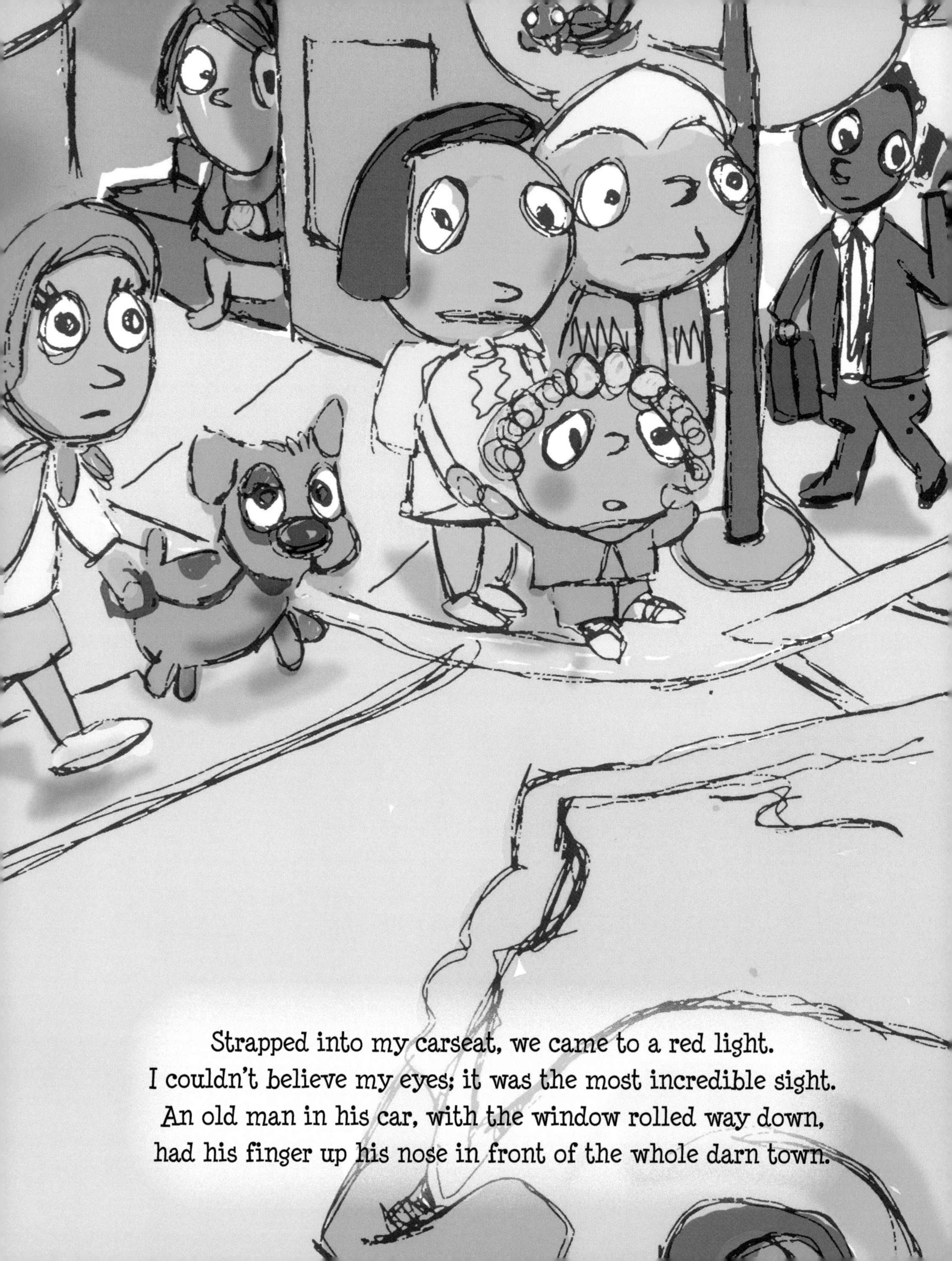

Strapped into my carseat, we came to a red light.
I couldn't believe my eyes; it was the most incredible sight.
An old man in his car, with the window rolled way down,
had his finger up his nose in front of the whole darn town.

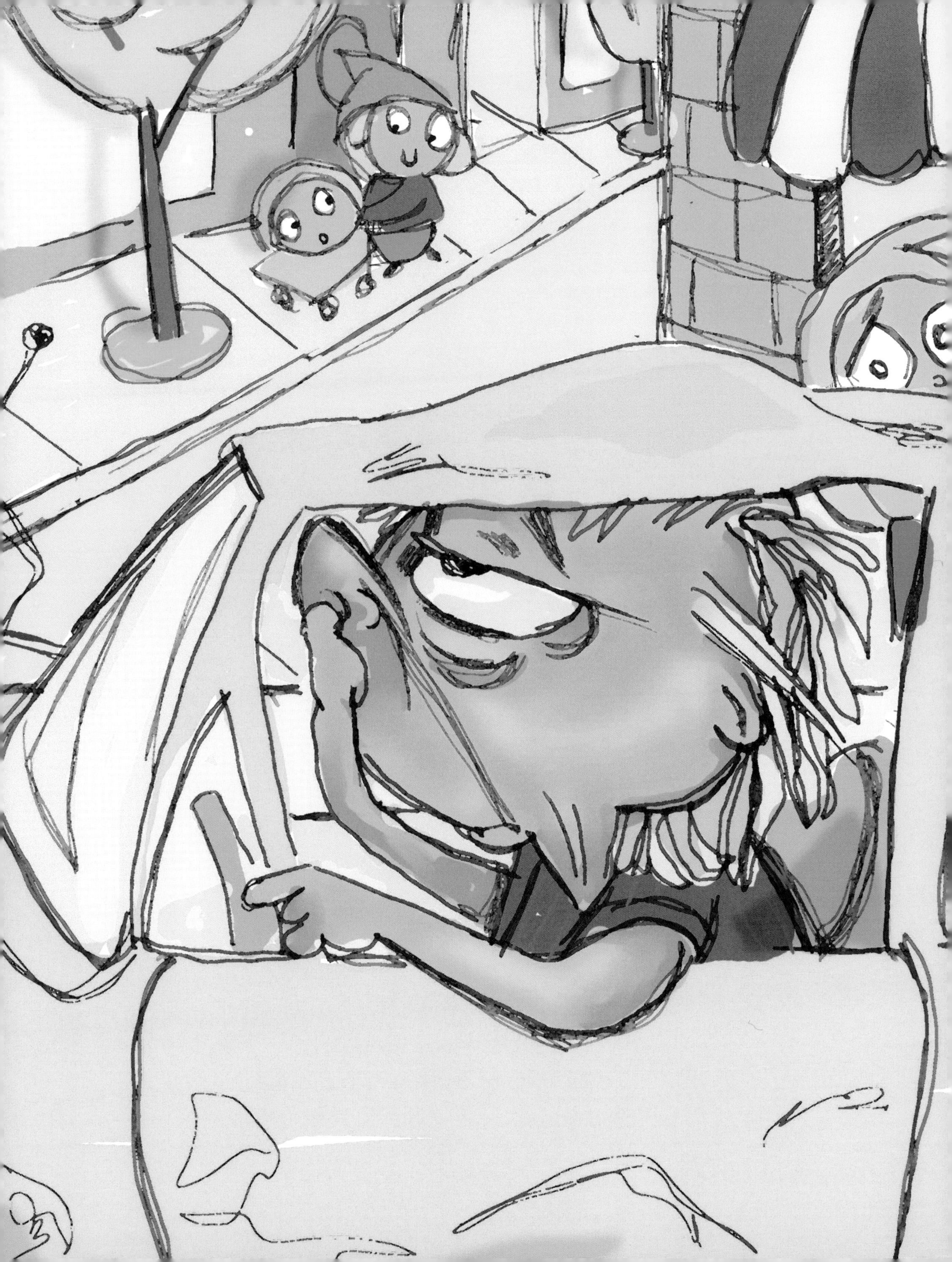

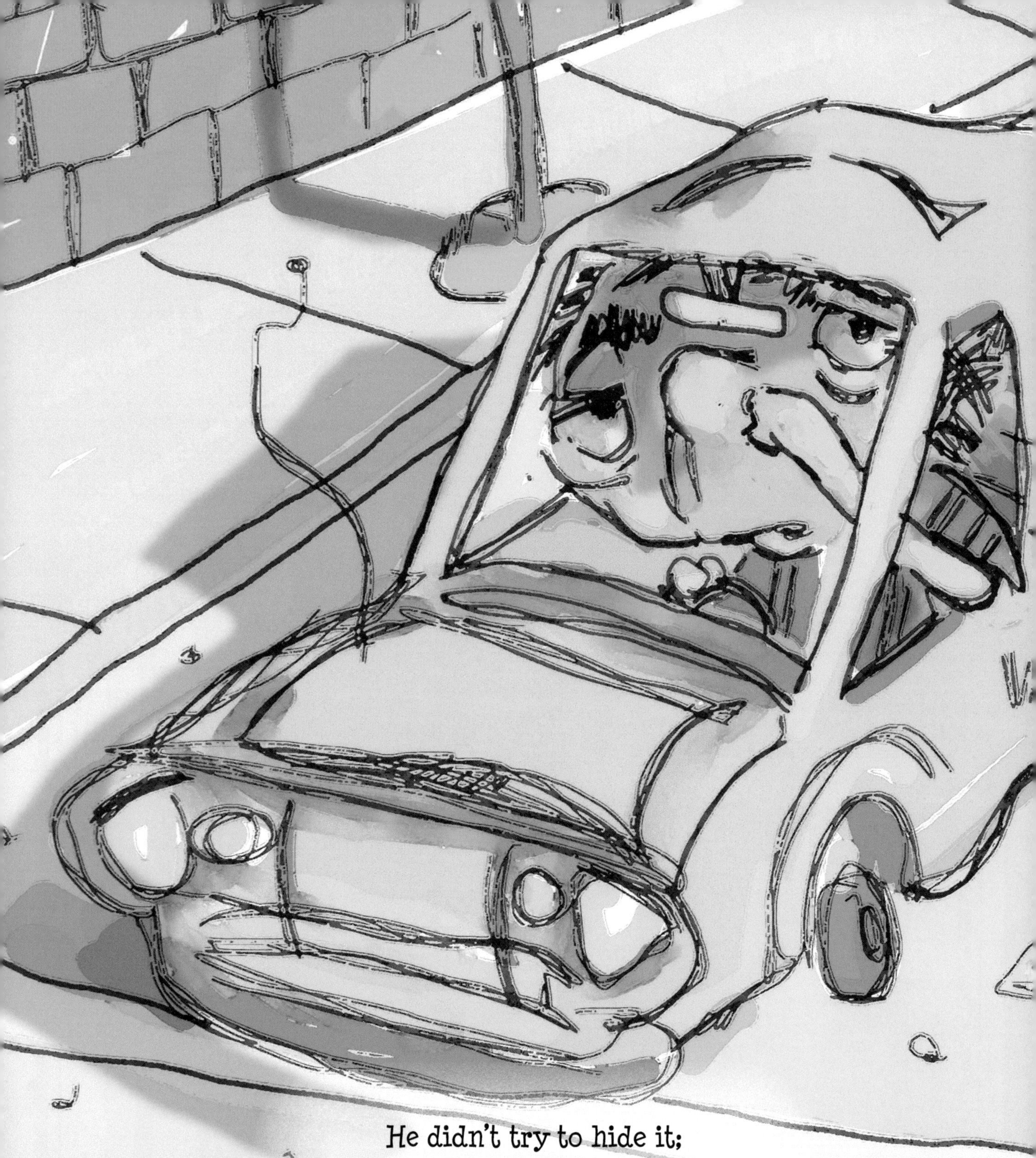

He didn't try to hide it;
he seemed to have no shame.
I smiled so big, was about to scream...
when the silly man took aim.

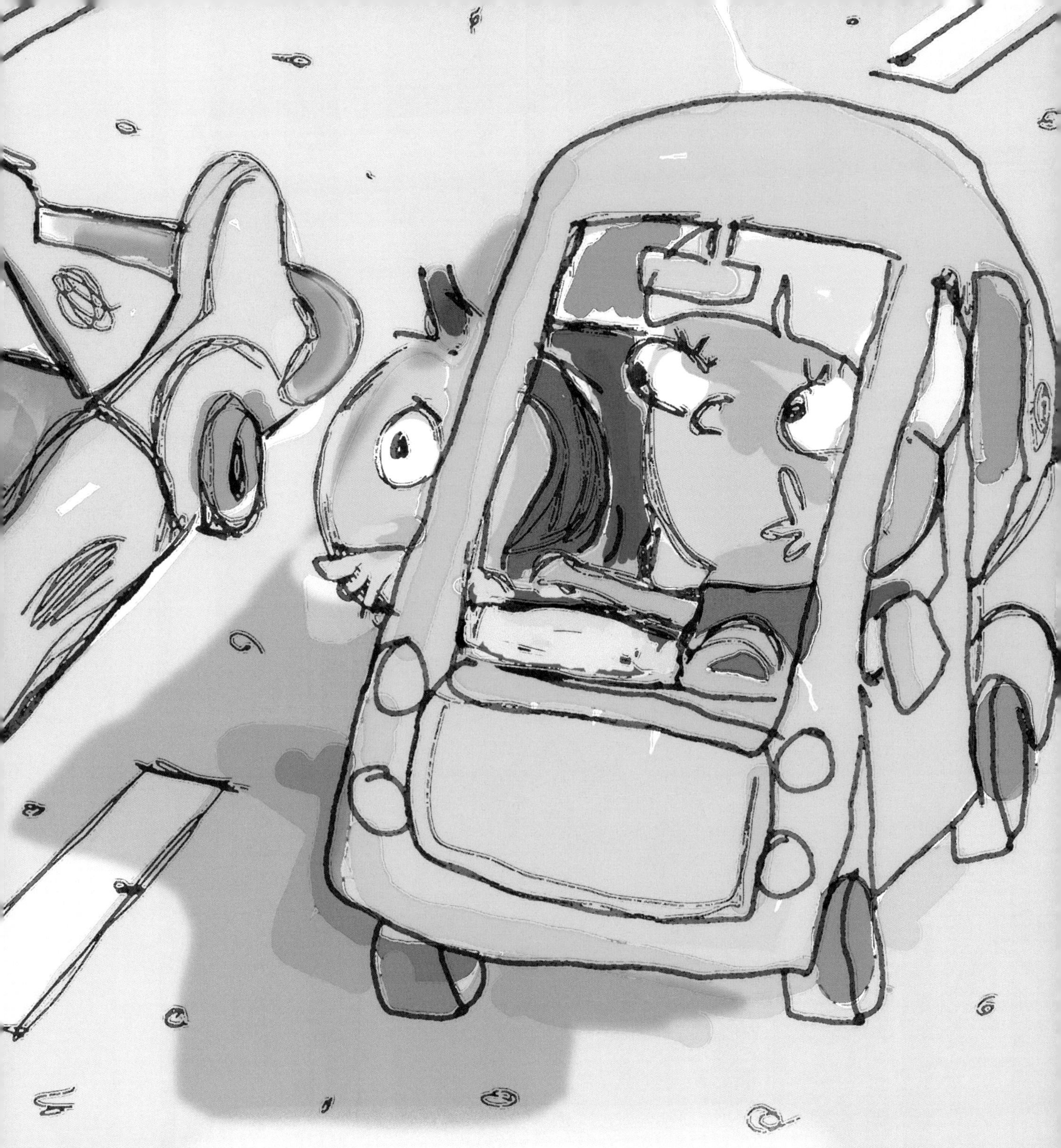

Before we discuss where it landed,
before I tell you what's next,
read on to find out how my Mom finally lost it—
with all this jazzy text.

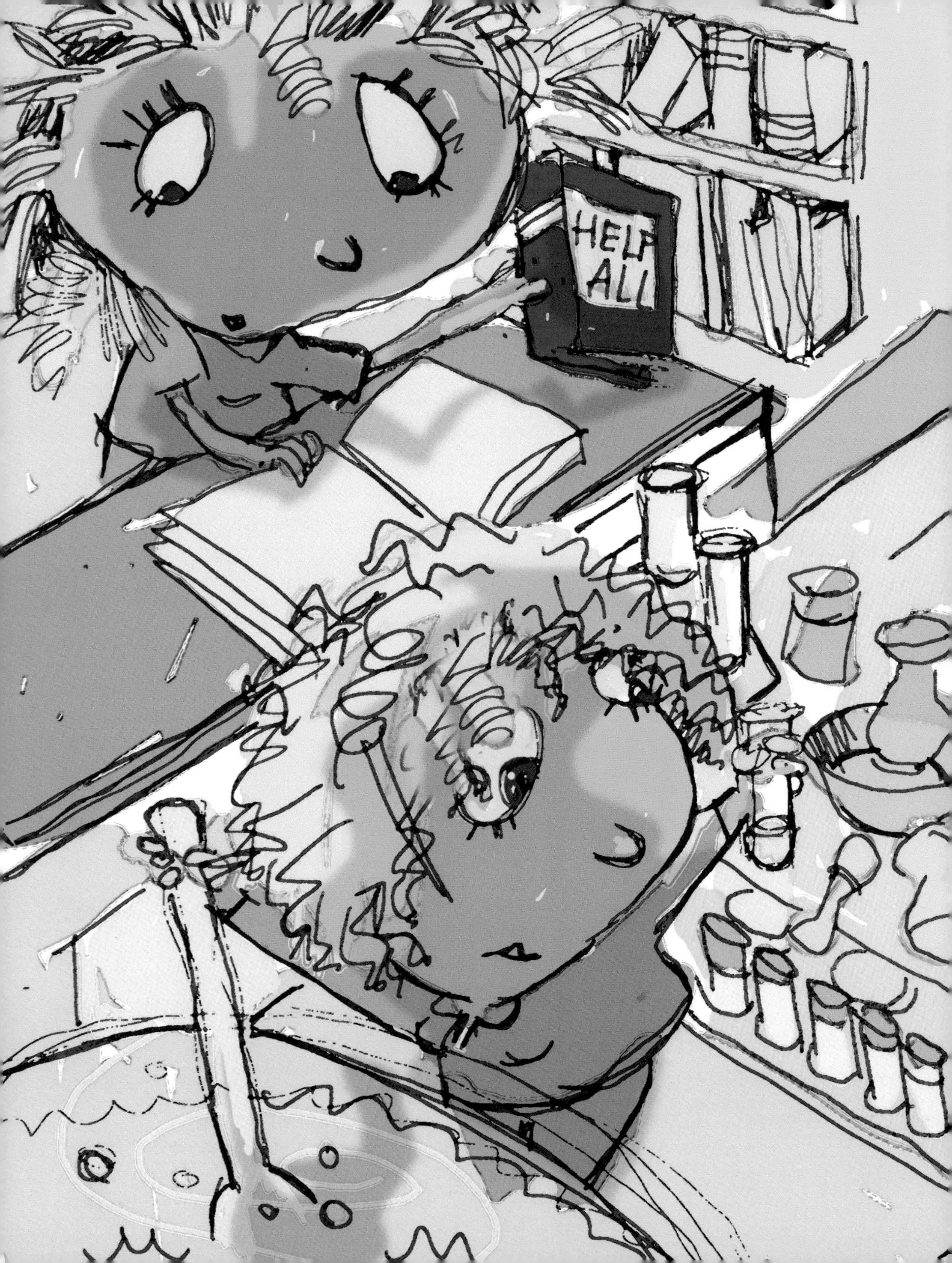
HELP ALL

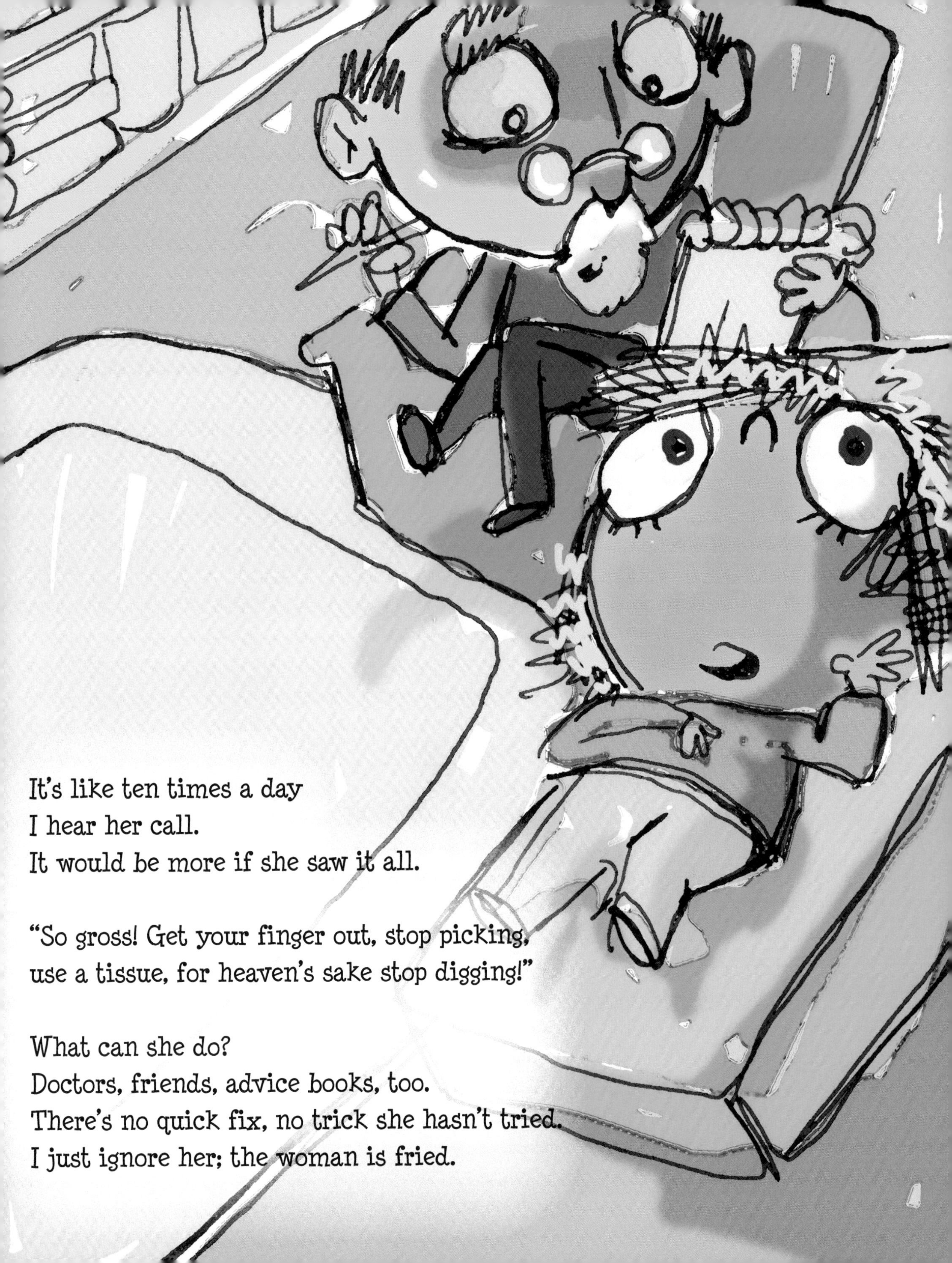

It's like ten times a day
I hear her call.
It would be more if she saw it all.

"So gross! Get your finger out, stop picking,
use a tissue, for heaven's sake stop digging!"

What can she do?
Doctors, friends, advice books, too.
There's no quick fix, no trick she hasn't tried.
I just ignore her; the woman is fried.

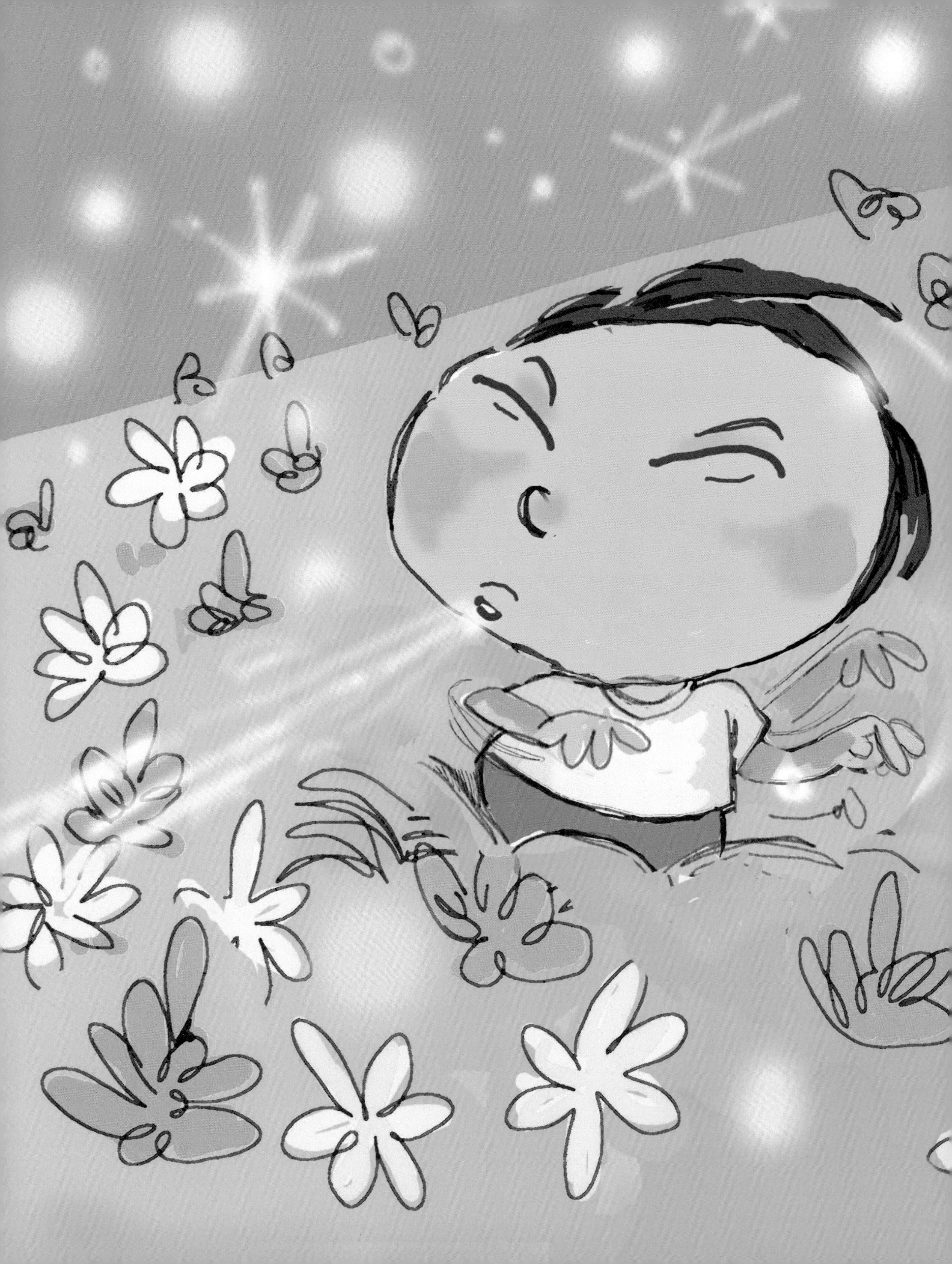

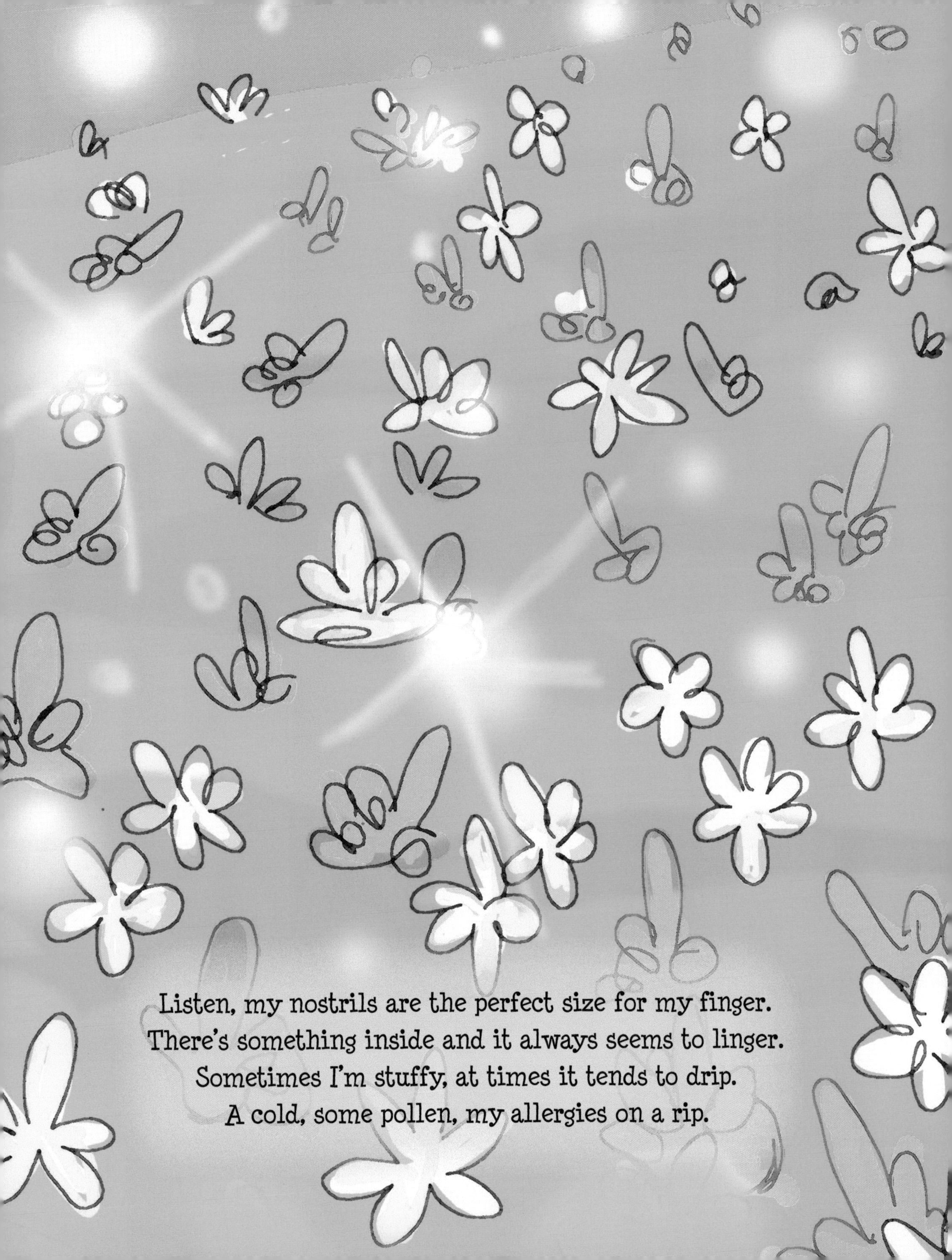

Listen, my nostrils are the perfect size for my finger.
There's something inside and it always seems to linger.
Sometimes I'm stuffy, at times it tends to drip.
A cold, some pollen, my allergies on a rip.

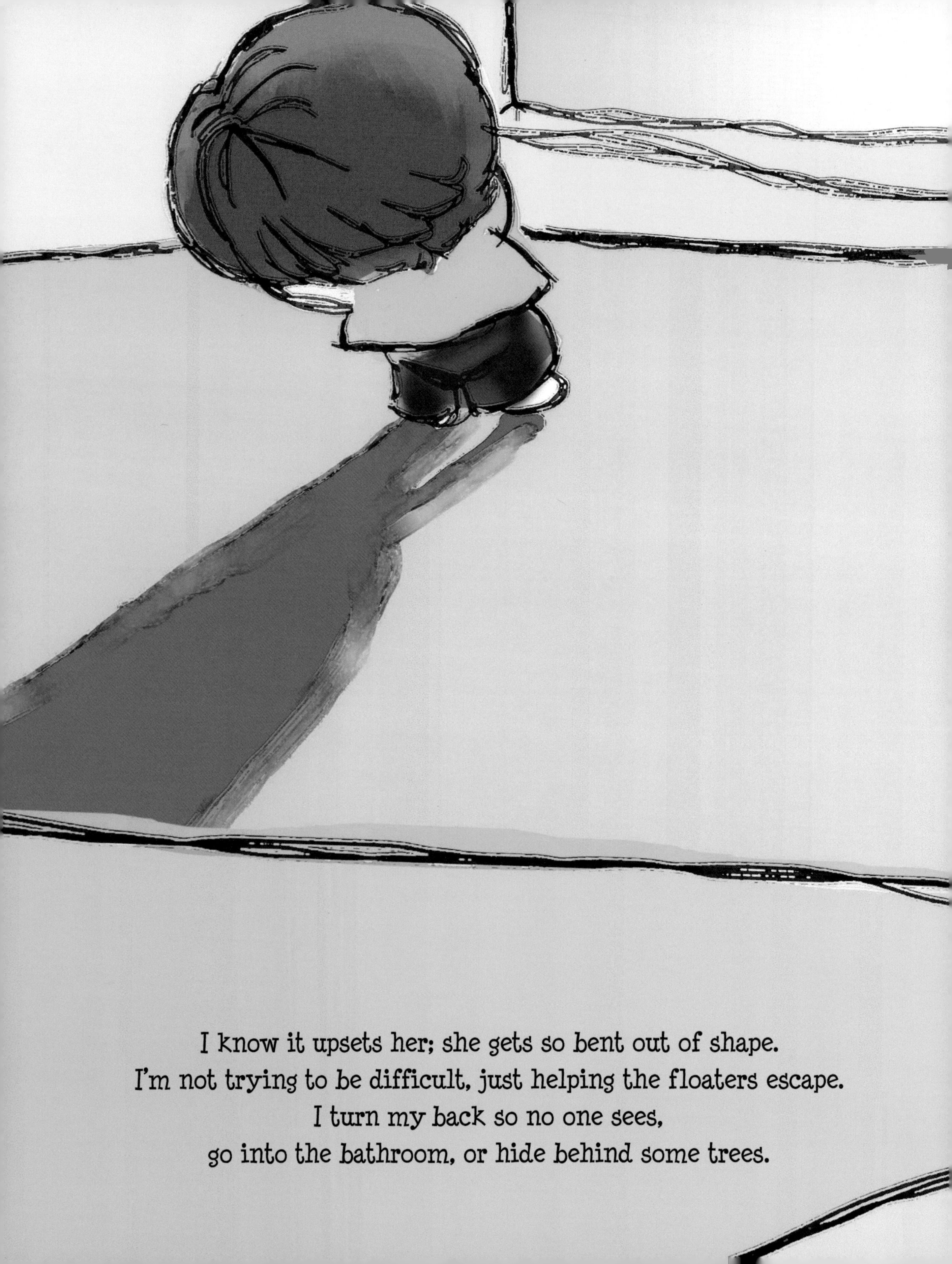

I know it upsets her; she gets so bent out of shape.
I'm not trying to be difficult, just helping the floaters escape.
I turn my back so no one sees,
go into the bathroom, or hide behind some trees.

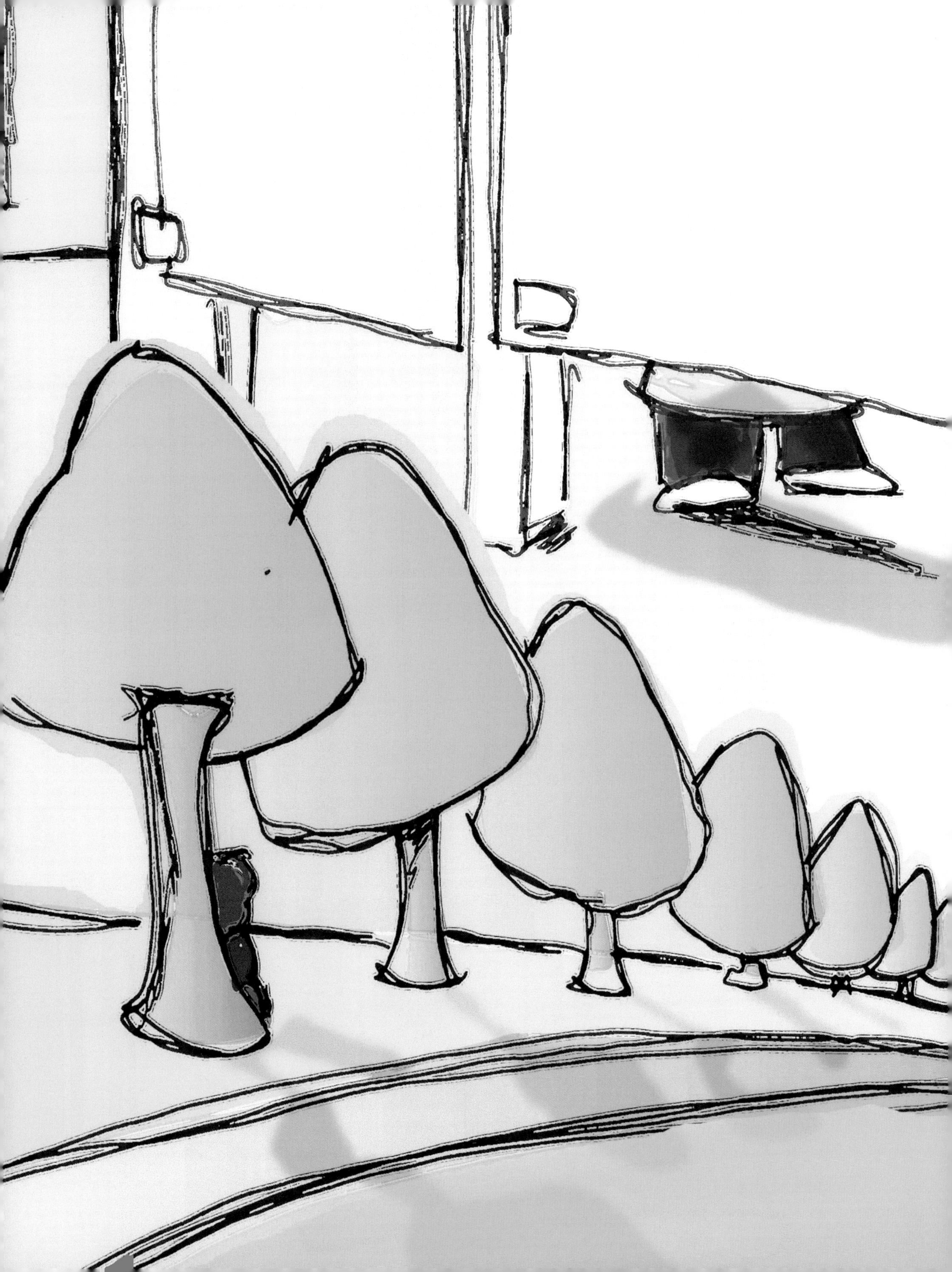

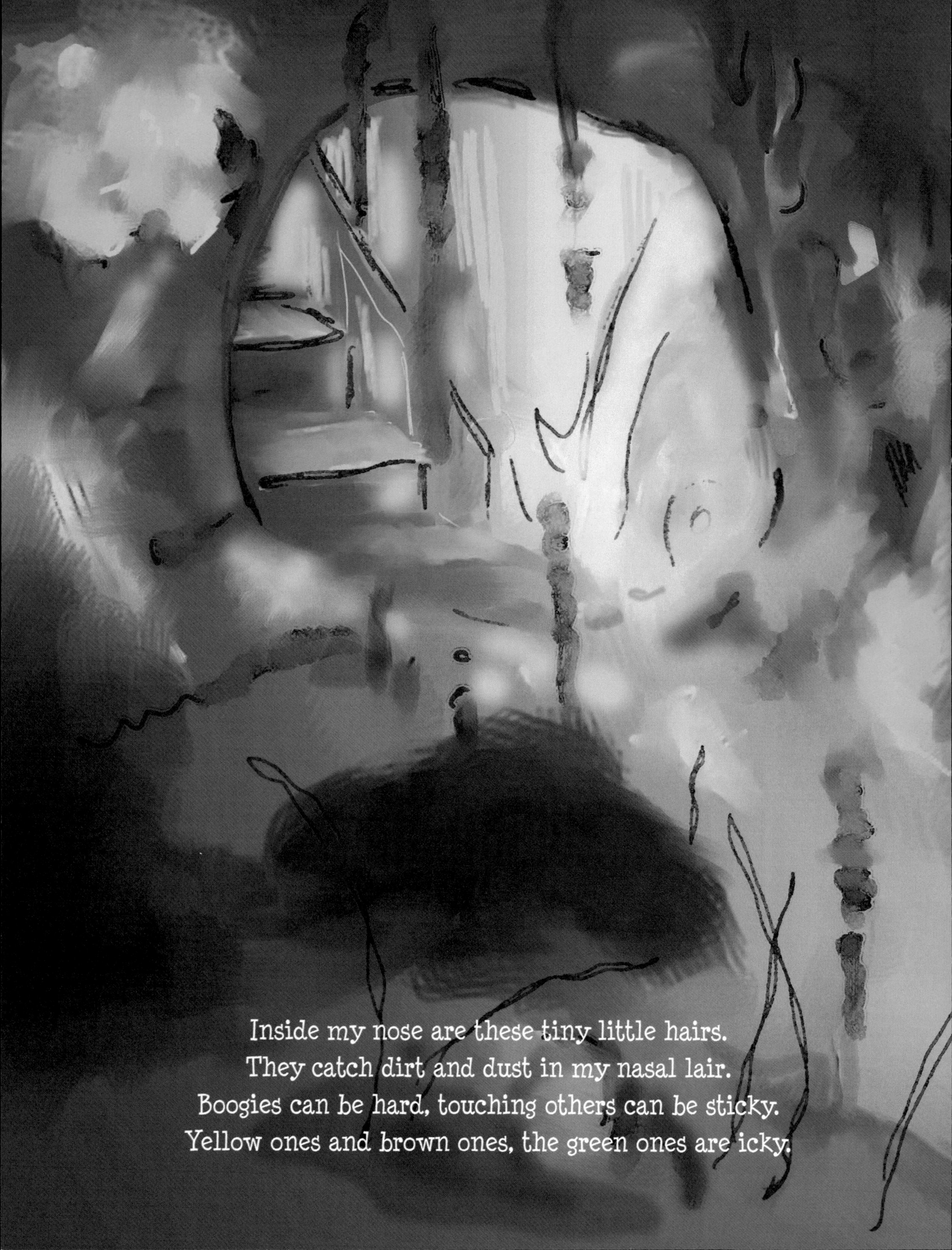

Inside my nose are these tiny little hairs.
They catch dirt and dust in my nasal lair.
Boogies can be hard, touching others can be sticky.
Yellow ones and brown ones, the green ones are icky.

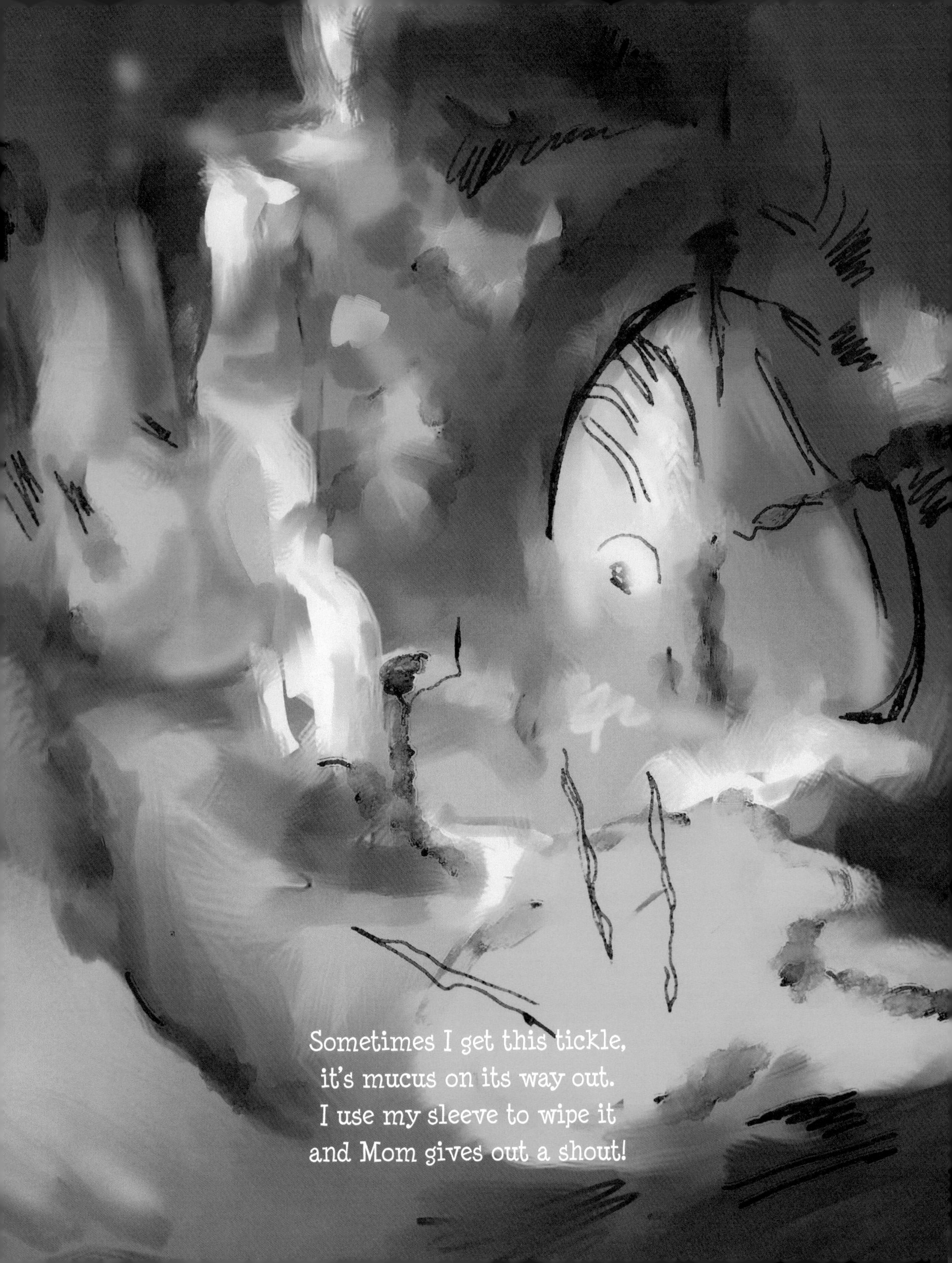

Sometimes I get this tickle,
it's mucus on its way out.
I use my sleeve to wipe it
and Mom gives out a shout!

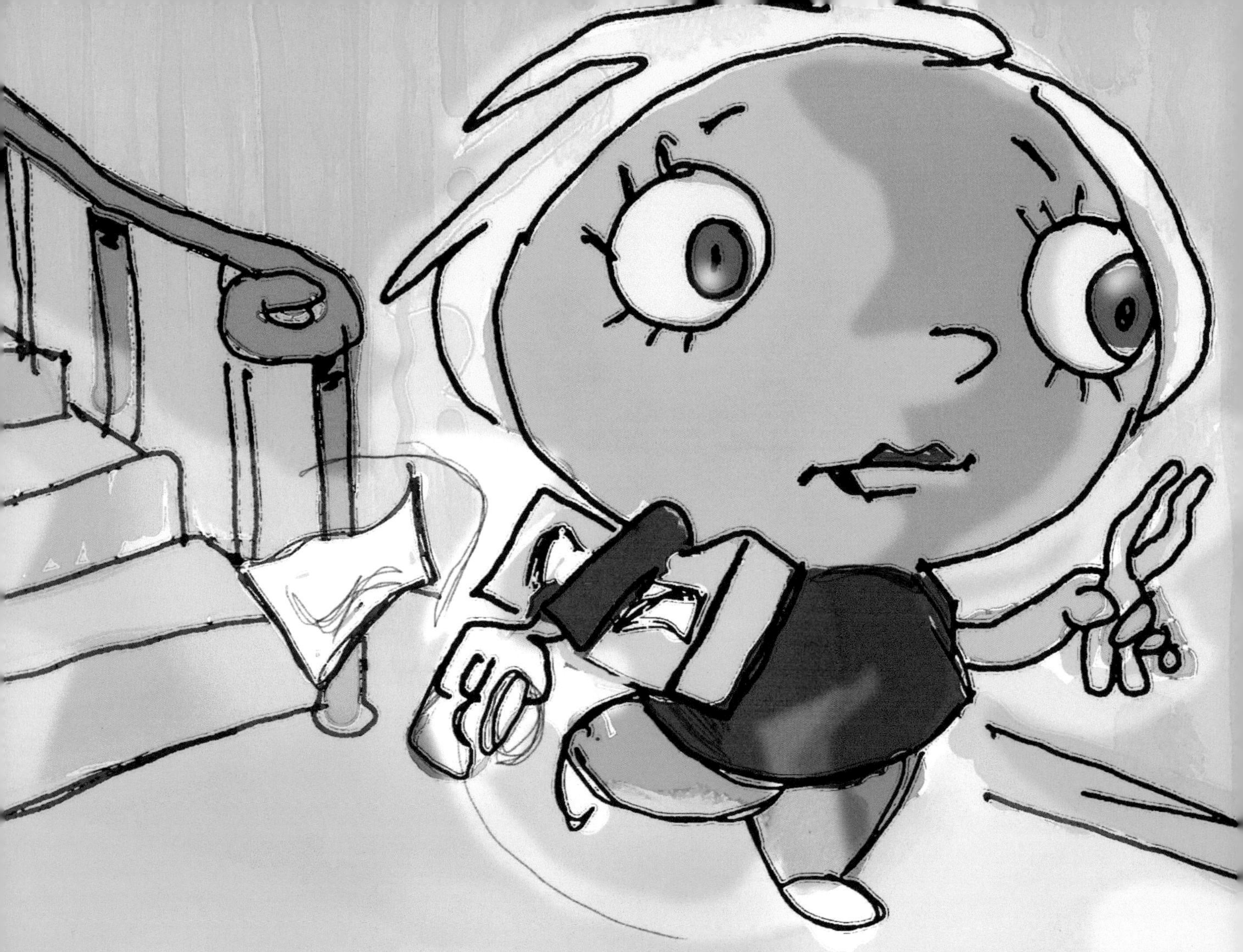

She gives me tissues for my pocket,
but I forget they are there.
She offers to pick it herself...
"Oh no, you wouldn't dare!"

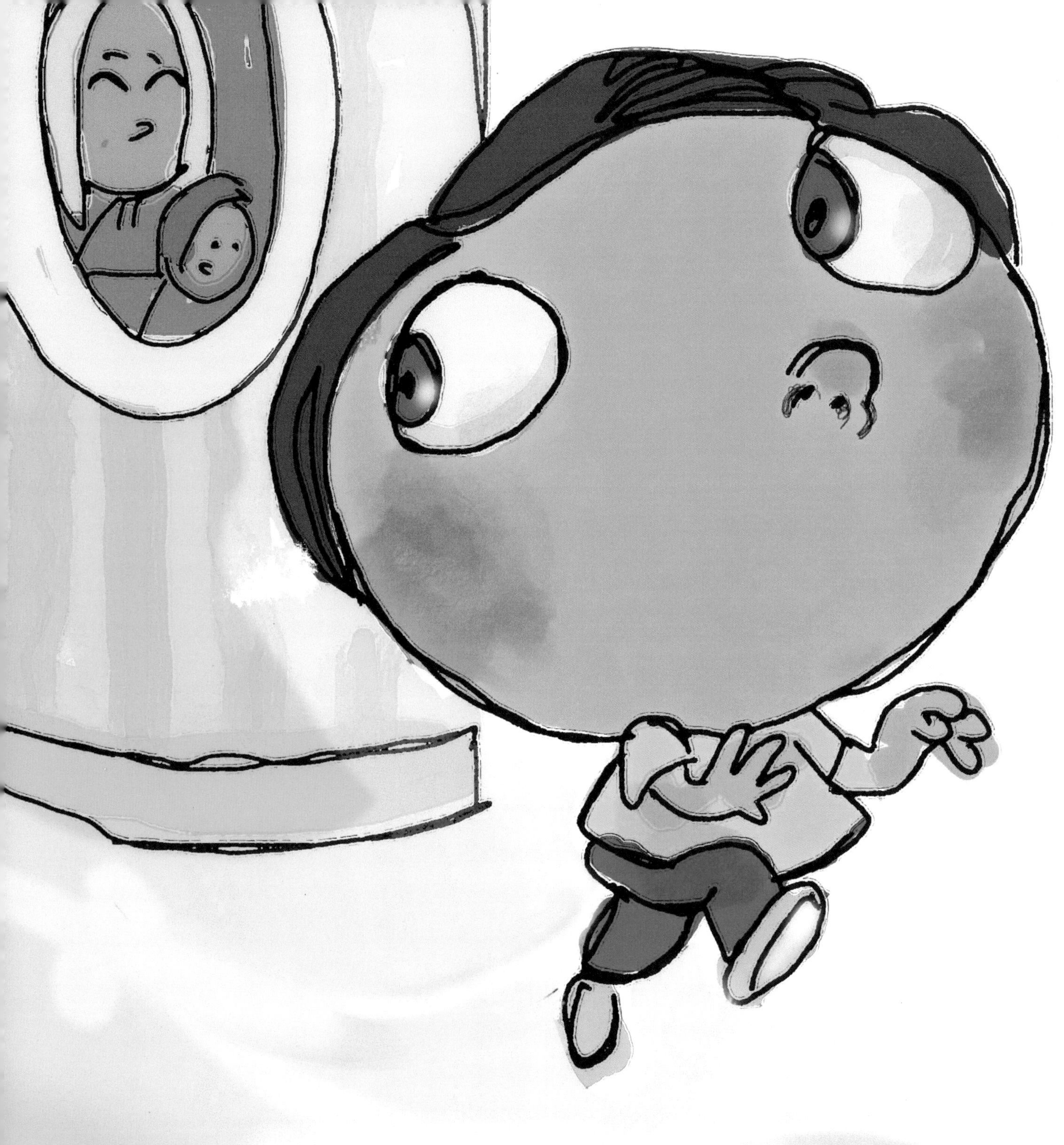

I truly don't know it's happening,
I play and pick at the same time.
I'm not hurting anyone.
It's multi-tasking, not committing a crime.

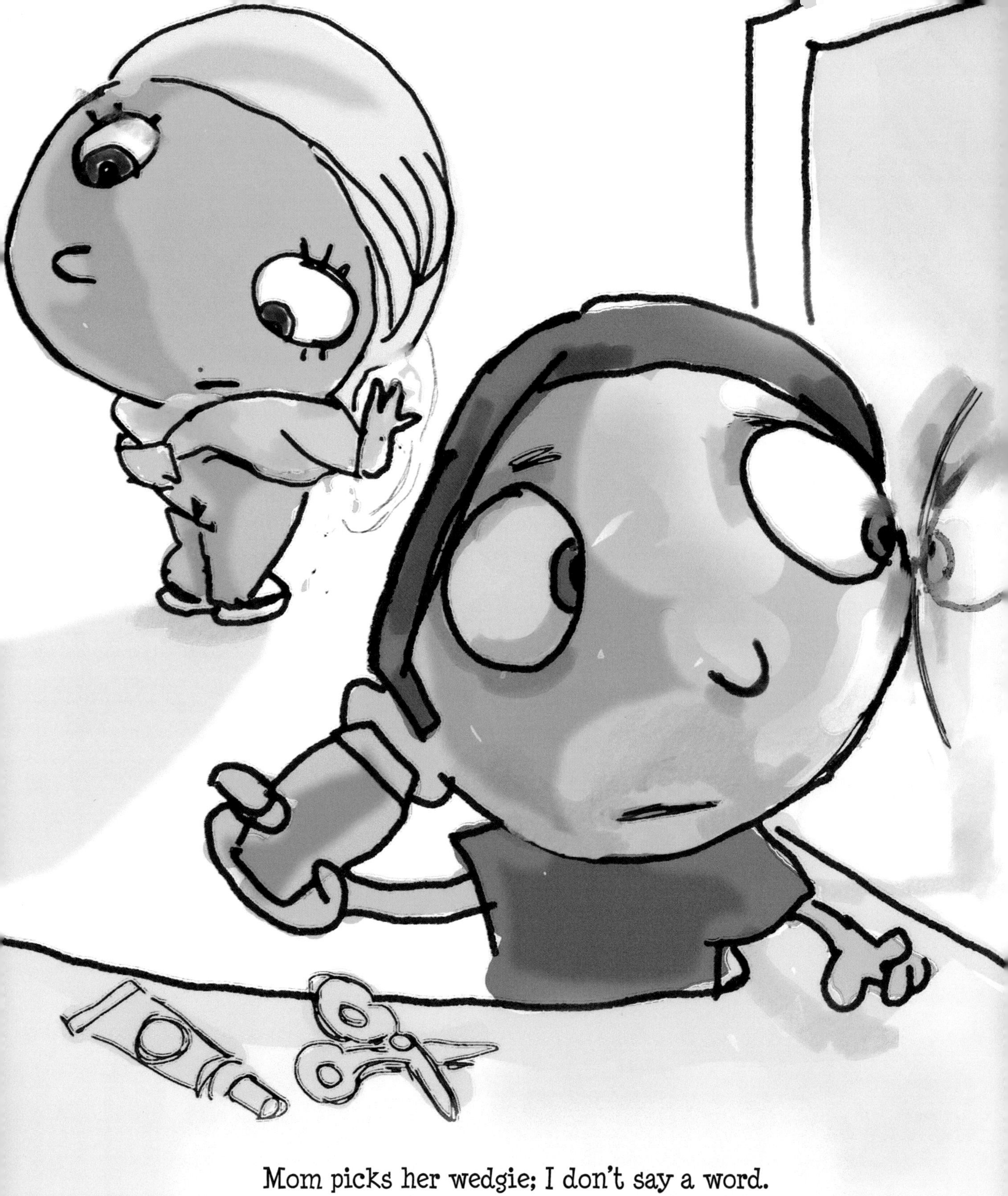

Mom picks her wedgie; I don't say a word.
Dad buzzes his ear hair; again I'm unheard.

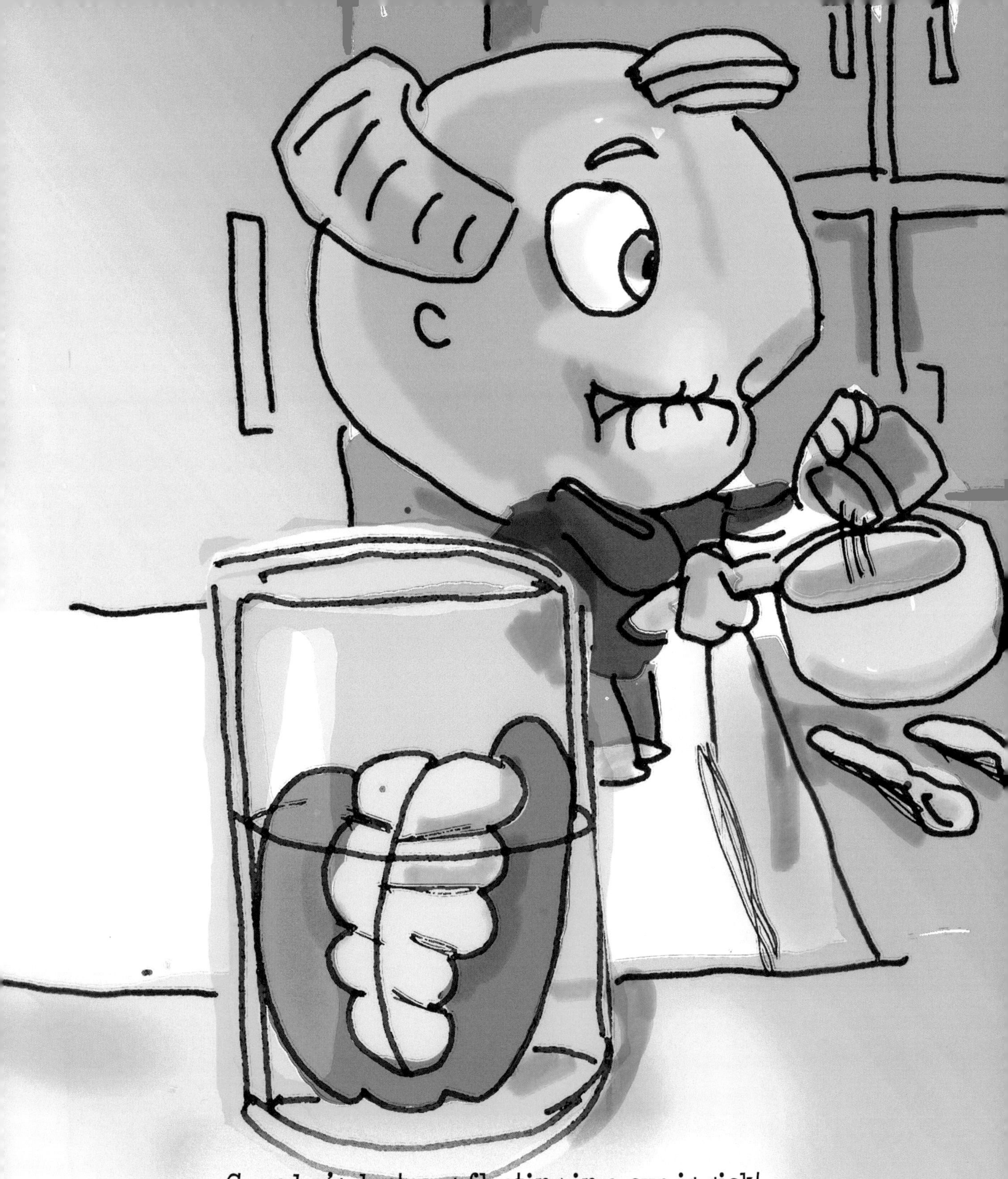

Grandpa's dentures floating in a cup is sick!
Leave my nose alone. I WILL PICK!!!!

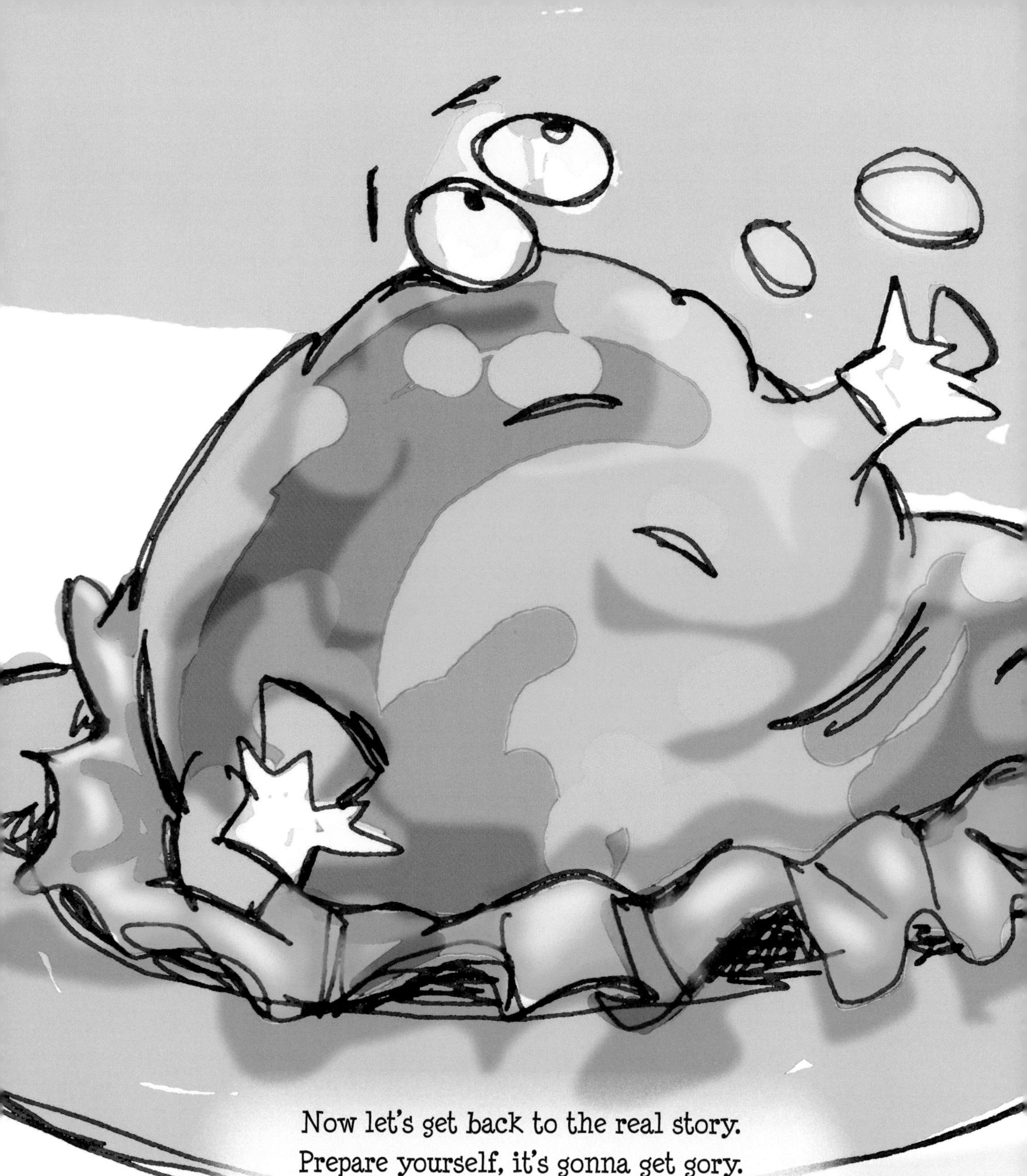

Now let's get back to the real story.
Prepare yourself, it's gonna get gory.
Remember that guy in the beat-up jalopy,
finger up his nose, his hair gray and sloppy?

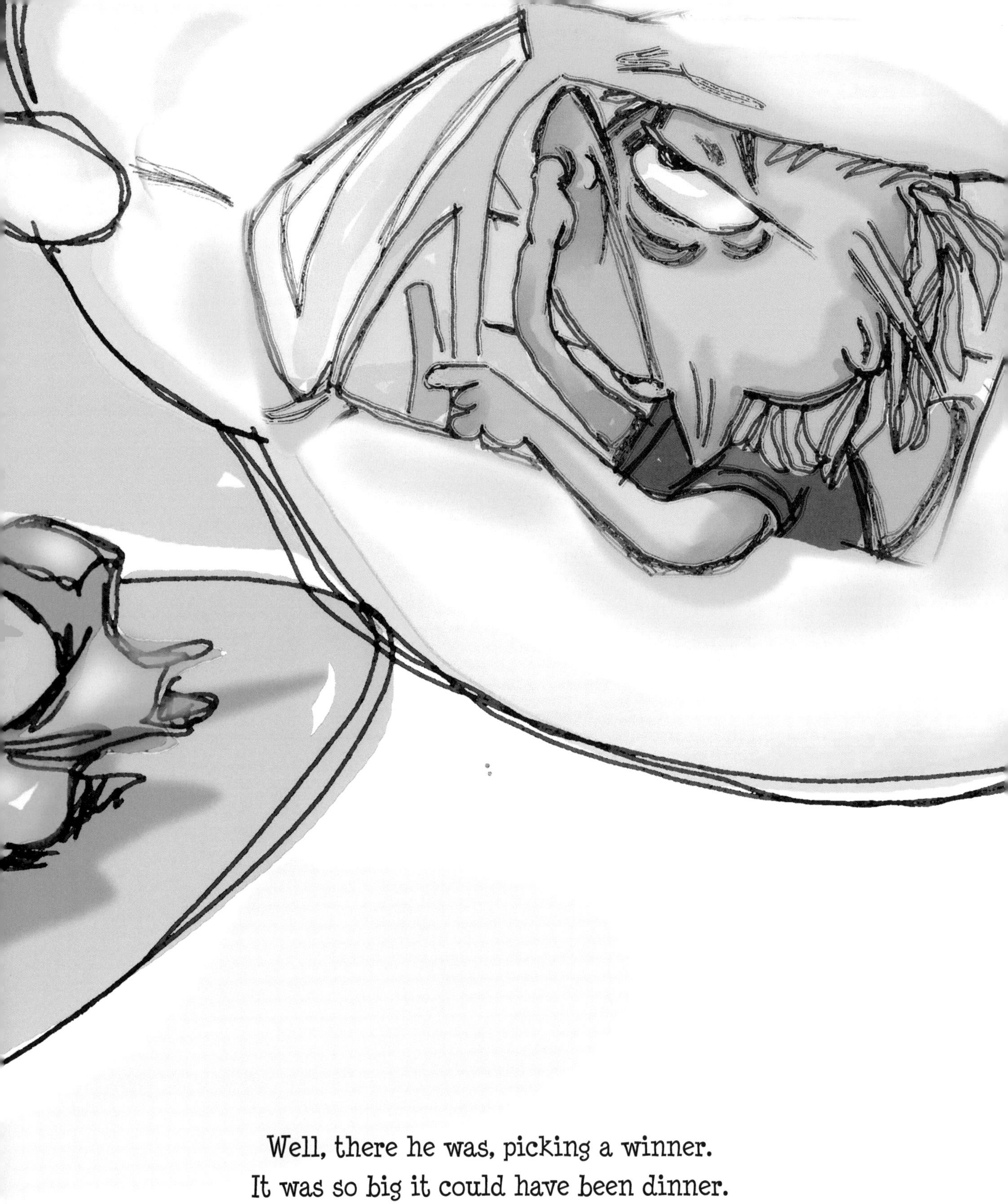

Well, there he was, picking a winner.
It was so big it could have been dinner.
When he pulled it out it gave us the shivers.

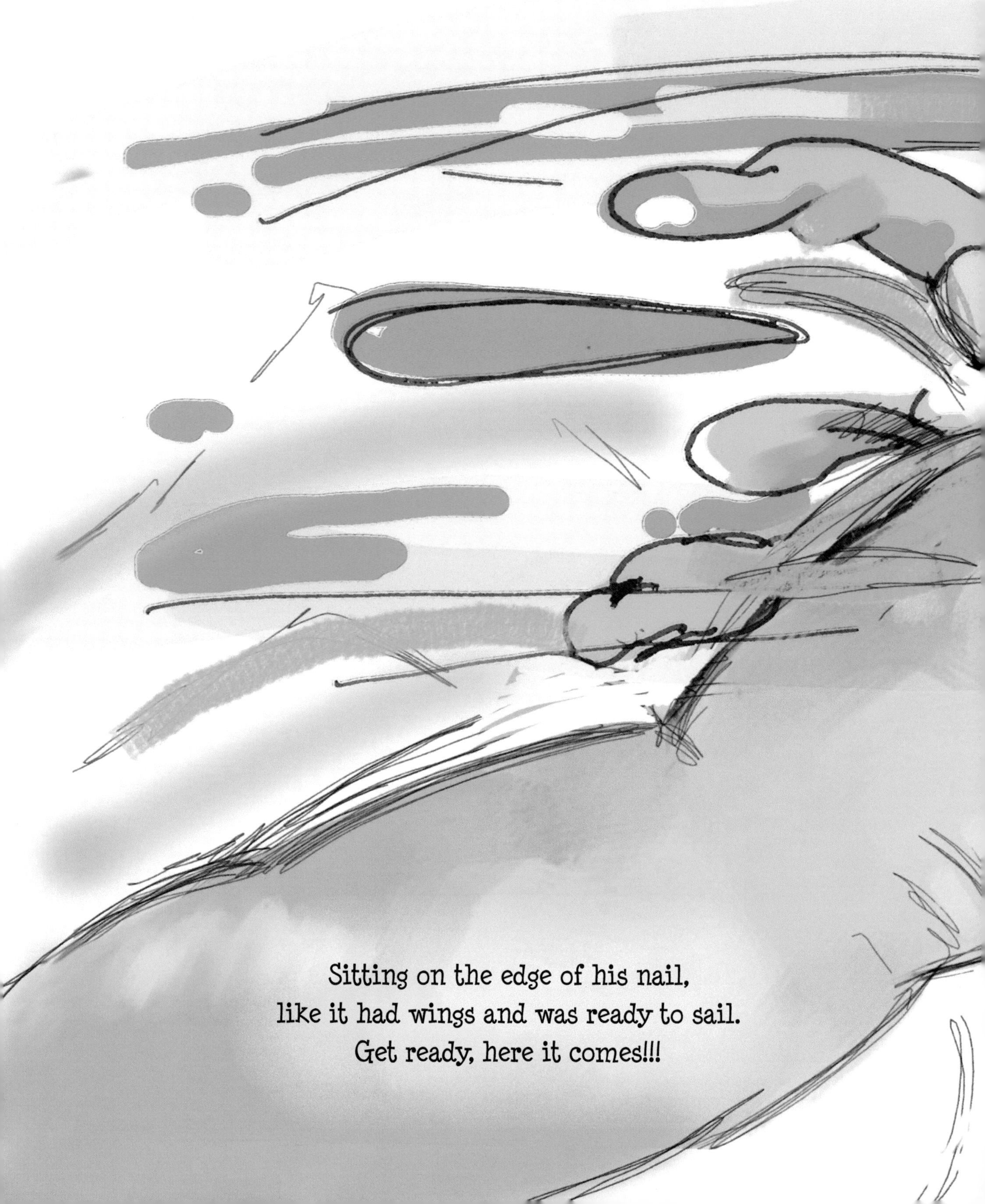

Sitting on the edge of his nail,
like it had wings and was ready to sail.
Get ready, here it comes!!!

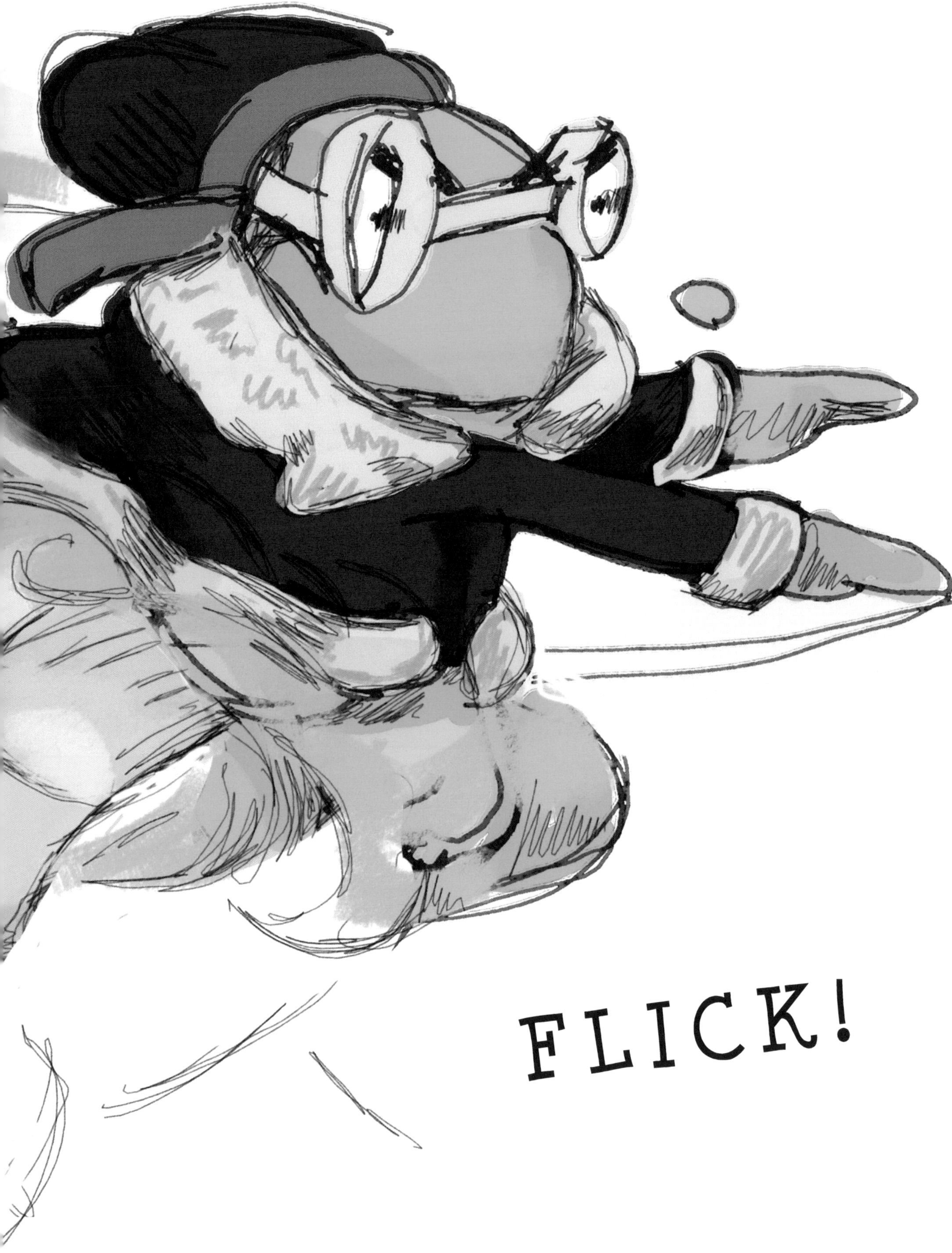

FLICK!

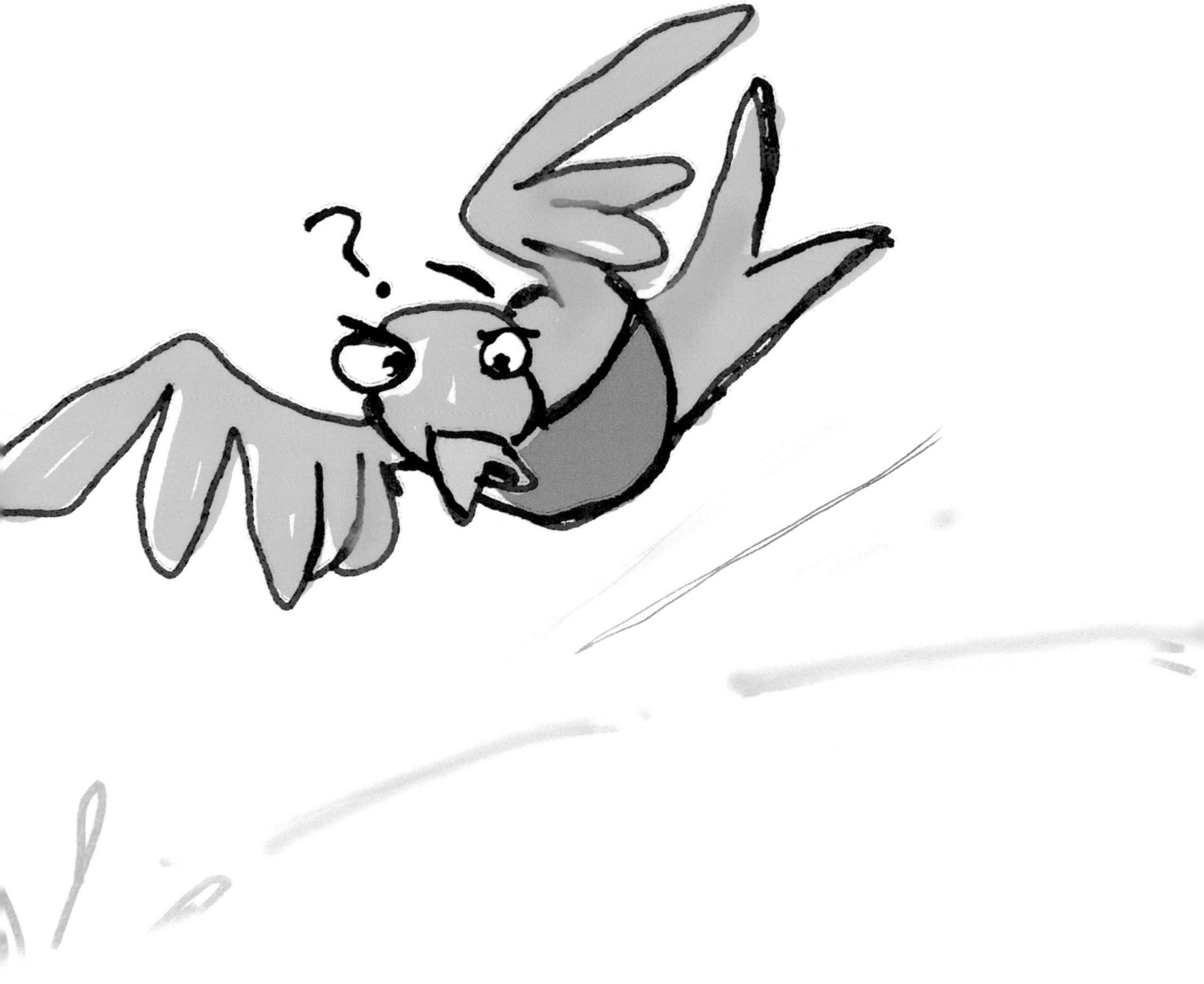
?

As fast as a sneeze, it flew through the air,
cut across traffic, and landed in my hair.
I screamed, "So gross! Get your finger out, stop picking,
use a tissue, for heaven's sake stop flicking!"

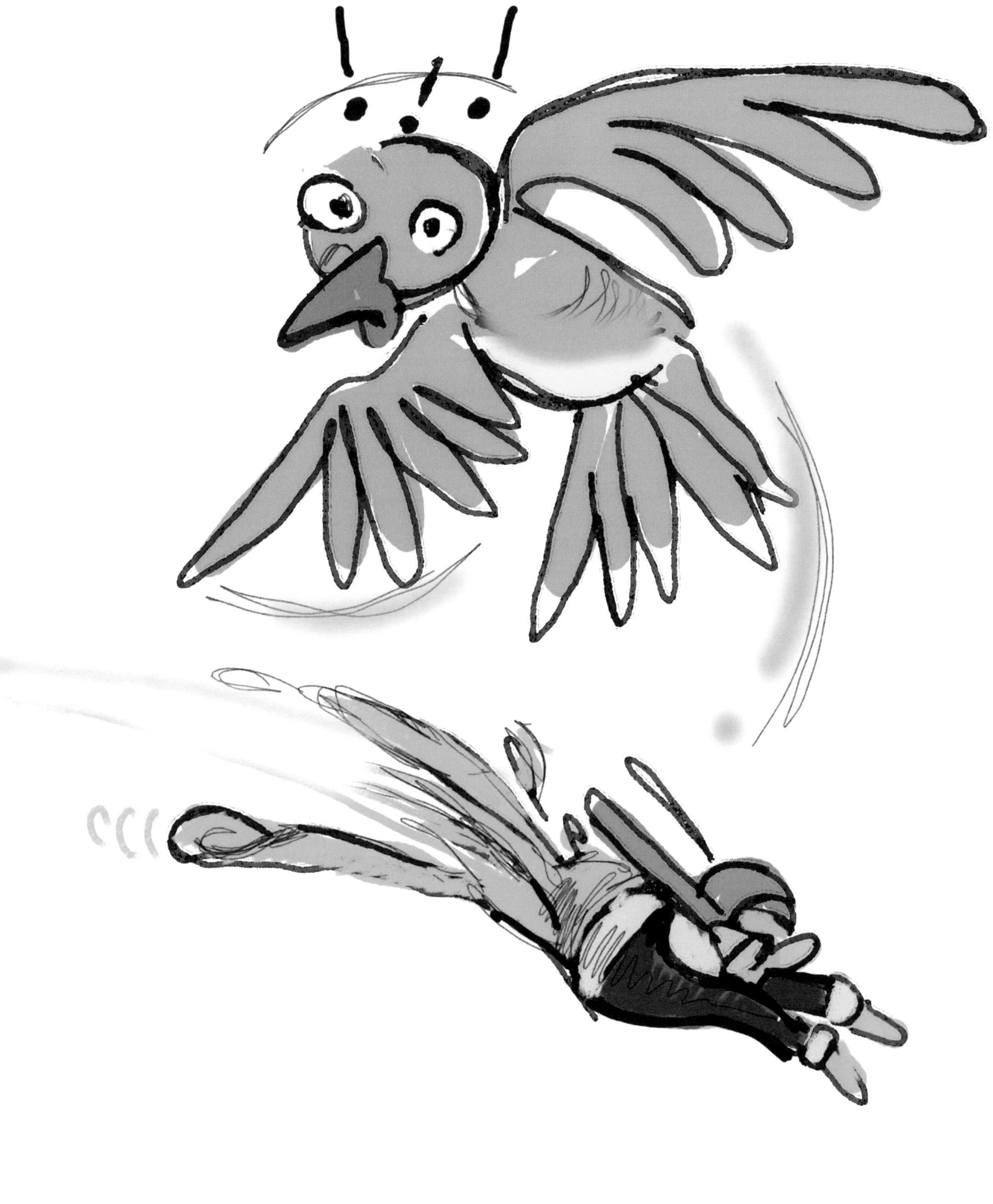

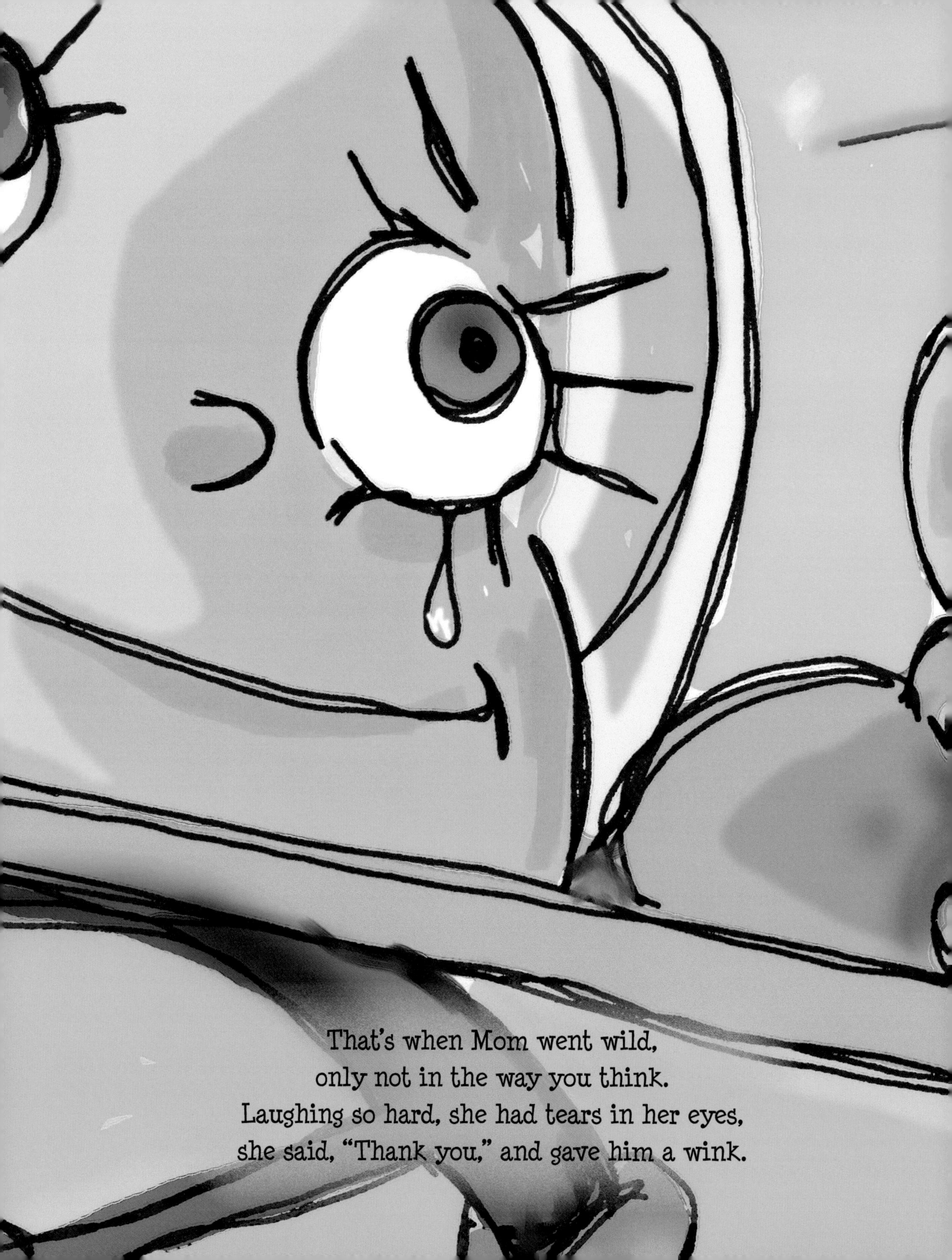

That's when Mom went wild,
only not in the way you think.
Laughing so hard, she had tears in her eyes,
she said, "Thank you," and gave him a wink.

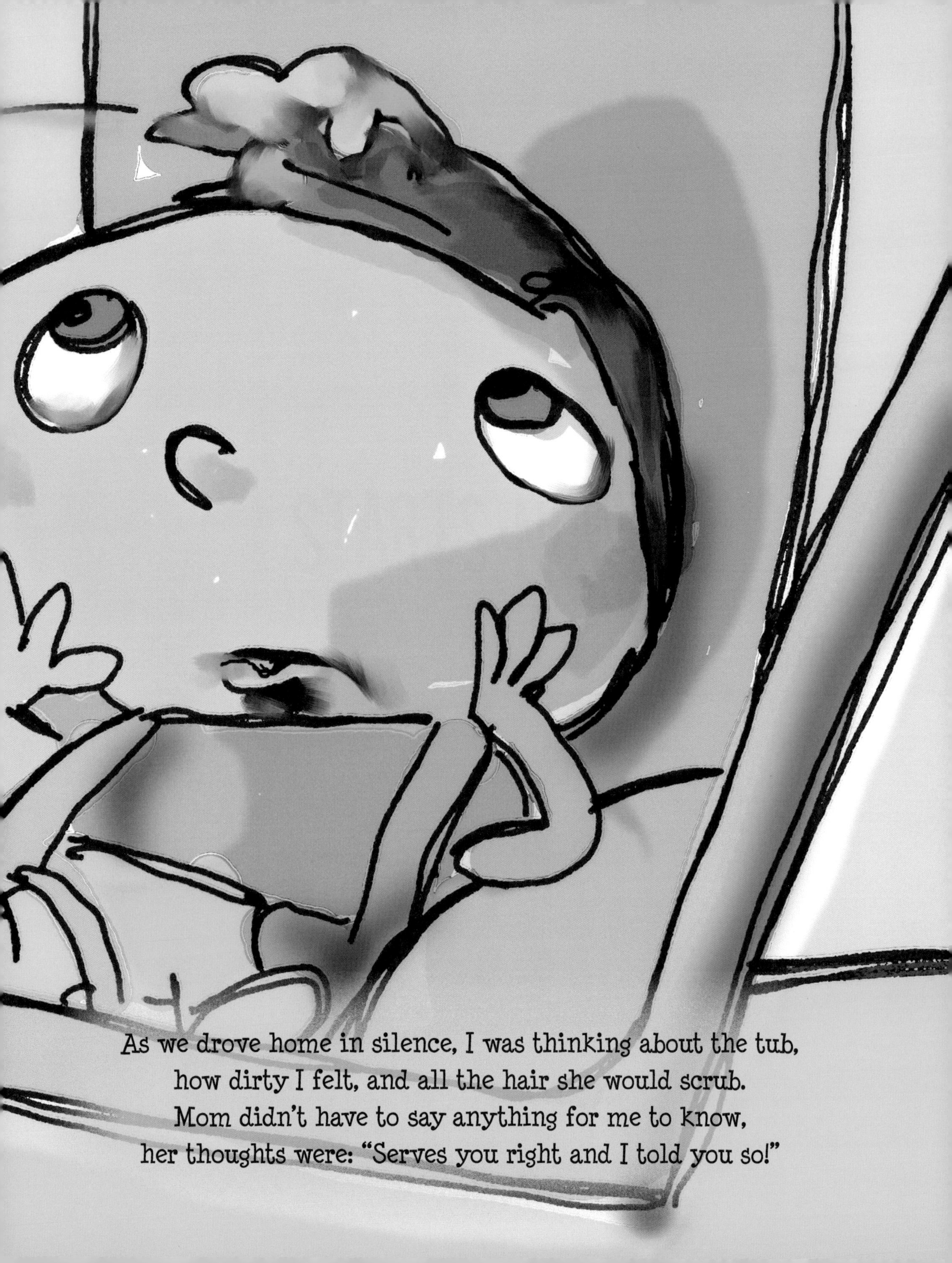

As we drove home in silence, I was thinking about the tub,
how dirty I felt, and all the hair she would scrub.
Mom didn't have to say anything for me to know,
her thoughts were: "Serves you right and I told you so!"

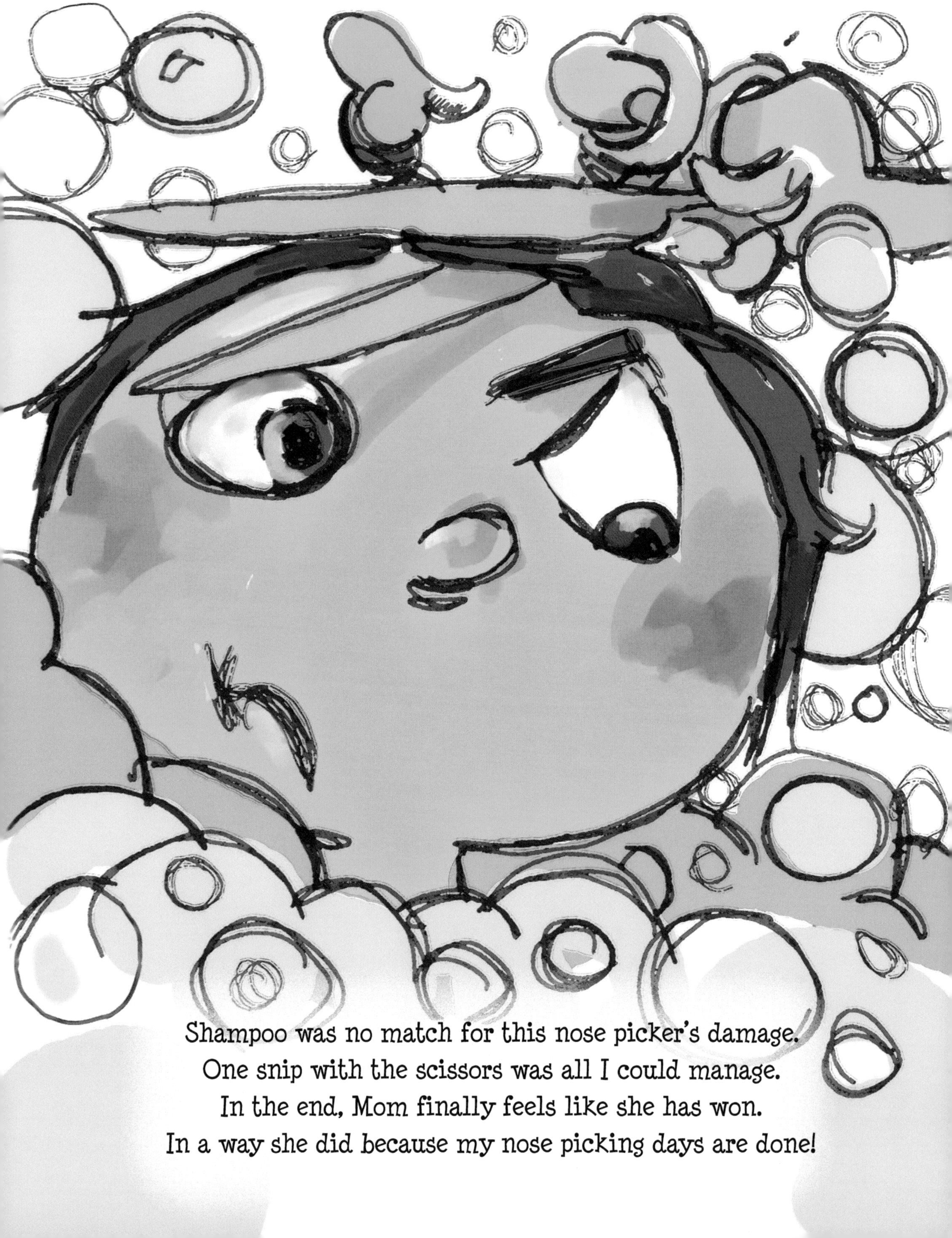

Shampoo was no match for this nose picker's damage.
One snip with the scissors was all I could manage.
In the end, Mom finally feels like she has won.
In a way she did because my nose picking days are done!

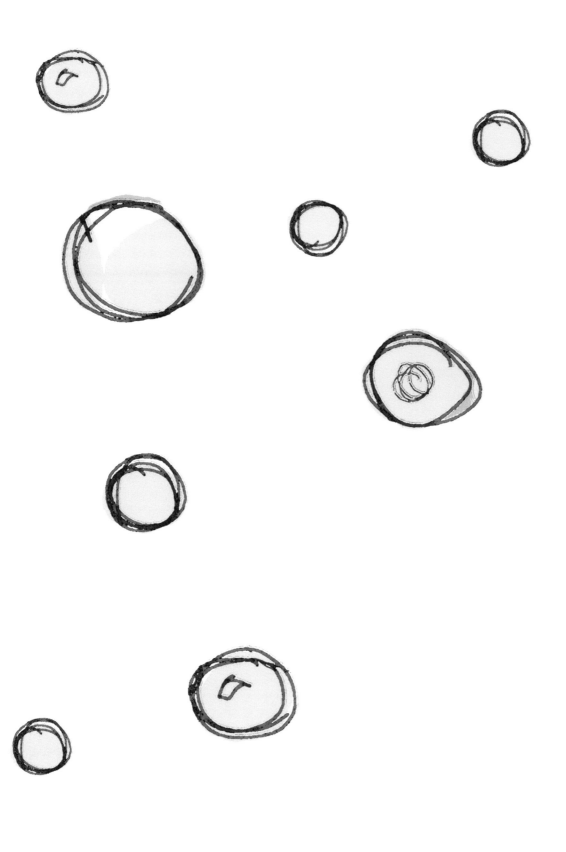

CPSIA information can be obtained
at www.ICGtesting.com
Printed in the USA
LVIC04n1553111115
462038LV00003B/7